REUNITED WITH DADDY

A DDlg Spanking Roleplay Erotic Romance

Sonia Lake

Copyright © 2020 Sonia Lake

All rights reserved

The characters and events portrayed in this book are fictitious. Any similarity to real persons, living or dead, is coincidental and not intended by the author.

No part of this book may be reproduced, or stored in a retrieval system, or transmitted in any form or by any means, electronic, mechanical, photocopying, recording, or otherwise, without express written permission of the publisher.

CONTENTS

CHAPTER ONE

Deep breath, Persy. You can do this.

I smooth my dress as I exit the taxi and take in the beautiful venue. It's early evening and the columns have been strung with small lights that cast a gentle warm glow over the sprawling, stately entrance.

Knowing Amanda and Billy, it's sure to be quite a wedding.

I met Amanda nearly four years ago when she moved to Albany. We met on an online DDlg forum and hit it off in person. Since, we've grown close, confiding in one another and sharing lots of fun, silly play dates.

Billy is a handful and a half — over six feet tall, nearly three hundred pounds of ornery, mischievous muscle. He and Amanda fell in love quickly after he hired her to be his private chef.

Guess the way to a man's heart really is through his stomach. Definitely true for Billy, at least.

The thought of enormous, hulking Billy doling out tender affection and harsh discipline has crossed my mind. I'd never try anything, of course — he's her Daddy Dom and only has eyes for Amanda.

Still, I can't help but be reminded of what I once had. My old Daddy, William, was my only real love. Dark and mysterious, cloaked in tattoos and sleek black clothing on top of his broad, muscular frame. An aloof look in his smoky brown eyes. From the outside, he looked cold and antisocial. But with me, he was the sweetest, most attentive Daddy Dom I could have asked for.

It's been nearly a decade since our split.

We met at the wrong time. Just young pups — me at 22 and him at 25. Our whirlwind romance was intense and deep for the two years we were together. Then he was promoted to a position in Salt Lake City. Randy, his brother, had opened a successful chain of weightlifting gyms. William was involved from the beginning, so he was a natural choice for western regional manager.

Every bone in my body ached when he left. It was impossible for me to go with him. Auntie Marie, the woman who raised me when my good-for-nothing parents headed south chasing dope, was dying of lung cancer. She needed constant care and I couldn't leave her. But part of my heart left with him that day and I still haven't healed.

Her illness was agony. Slow, brutal decay from the inside out. It ate away at her for eight years until she passed. Two years ago, now…it's as if it happened a lifetime ago, and like it just happened yesterday. An aching loss.

It was a relief when she died. For all the love she'd given me, I was glad to know that her suffering was finally over.

The pain of her absence was mine alone to bear. She's finally free from it all.

Get it together, Persy, I chide harshly as emotions clog my throat. Why do I always do this? I feel a twinge of sadness and then every painful memory bubbles to the surface. I shake it off, setting my sights on the crowded foyer.

You're capable. You're safe. Old affirmations from a lifetime ago ring through my ears. I'm not sure if I remember his voice correctly, but the words still bring me comfort as I snake through the crowd.

The venue is filled with elegant splendor — cream and gold accents decorate the long procession to the altar. I grab a seat near the middle on Amanda's side.

It's a beautifully decorated wedding, but the atmosphere is relatively relaxed. Seating is open. After the ceremony, we'll have cocktails and then a buffet dinner and dancing. Amanda assured me that I wouldn't embarrass her with my lack of refinery. She and Billy waged a bet about whose side of the family will cause a drunken scene at the reception. Don't sweat it, she laughed.

Throngs of guests file into the seats and I take them in. Regular, unglamorous people in their best outfits, wide eyed and smiling at the gorgeous scene. As I suspected, Billy's family is humongous. His father, uncle, and brothers are nearly as big as him. The front row on Billy's side looks like the bench at a pro football game.

Amanda's side is sparser. She's a wonderful friend, but she doesn't take to many people. I'm grateful that I'm here to support her.

My heart wrenches as Billy takes his place at the altar. They'd decided to ditch the bridesmaids and groomsmen after Billy's brothers duked it out about where they'd hypothetically stand. Amanda confided that she was relieved. Her mother was flying out from California, but only after some cajoling on Amanda's part.

"I'm nobody's to give away but mine," she'd told me with fiery conviction. Tears well in my eyes as her entrance music starts and she makes her way down the aisle in her sleek, silky wedding dress. It hugs her gorgeous curves perfectly.

By the time the ceremony starts, I'm bawling. Their devotion to one another is so clear it fills the room. Their love is palpable in the air.

God damn it. A pit opens up in my stomach and the sadness consumes me. A dry knot closes my throat.

I've never exactly had a right rein on my emotions. I've always been compassionate and sensitive, which are not easy traits to have in this world. It's easy for me to be swallowed up in darkness, unable to see anything beyond the suffering.

Since Auntie passed, it's been even worse. Innocuous things will trigger intense crying spells. The music swells and my entire body feels gross and jittery, like I'm full of acidic spiders instead of human meat.

Go. Go. Go. My heart is beating aggressively in my temples as my breathing quickens. Every cell in my body is screaming for me to run. I have to find a private place to weep some of this bitter, gnawing pain out of my system.

I smile big at Amanda and Billy as they walk down the aisle arm-in-arm. Jealousy roils in my gut no matter how hard I try to bat it away. Once they're out, people start to rise and I book it out of the venue into the darkness outside.

The cool air chills the anxious sweat beading on my brow and down my spine. Should've grabbed my coat. A shiver passes over me.

The cold braces me and draws me back into the present moment. *Anchor.* It's a skill my therapist taught me.

I walk slowly down the marble steps, focusing on the sensation of each footfall. Smelling the sweet, clean scent on the air. Breathing it deep down into my belly then exhaling completely, pushing out some of that tension.

I'm here now. I'm okay. The words fail to comfort me. My palm grazes over the coarse shrubbery and I focus on the sensation against my skin as I walk along the side of the building.

It's not about you tonight.

I shouldn't feel this way. Fuck. That only makes me feel worse. A tear slips down my cheek and I curse quietly as I brush it away.

Thank god I was always hopeless with makeup. Now all I have to hide are my swollen, red-ringed eyes. I press the heel of my hand against my eye and sigh at the cool touch. My hands are always cold, but out here in just a cocktail dress, they could serve as ice packs.

Chin up, girlie, Auntie's voice rings in my ears. I smooth my hands over my face as if that'll push all the nagging thoughts from my head. With a deep breath I square my shoulders, set my face, and head back towards the entrance.

There's a faint clinking sound as I approach the first wide marble column. As I turn the corner, I stop dead in my tracks.

William is drawing the lit cigarette from his lips as wisps of smoke cloud the air around him.

William? It can't be.

His eyes go wide when he sees me and I'm sure at any moment I'll wake in my bed, far away from this cruel dream.

CHAPTER TWO

William

Ugh. Fucking weddings.

Don't get me wrong, this one's okay. Billy and Amanda are good people. They've managed to put a party together that's stylish without being garish and overdone. My sister's wedding last year looked like a Pinterest board threw up in a fire hall.

That ceremony sucked all the air out of the room. It was clear how much they love each other, and like a selfish bastard, I thought about Persephone.

My little goddess, lost long ago. Being back in Albany flooded me with memories of her, of our relationship. Earlier, I swear I smelled her shampoo on the air. Must finally be losing my fucking mind.

I think back to my first meeting with Billy as I anxiously wait for the proper cue to get the fuck outta this room and get some nicotine into my system. I don't think a craving is causing that anxious jitter in my hand, though.

Billy came into my gym when he was competing at a strongman event in Salt Lake. He walked in and declared that he'd arrived, everyone will need to hand over their plates so he can "manage a decent fucking warm-up."

When I approached him to find out who this arrogant bastard was, cursing at my members, he slapped me on the back and told me he just got his girl's engagement ring. And he's gonna win today's meet.

"Gonna have rug burn on my dick between the judges tuggin' and my sweet little wifey," he said with a hearty laugh. There was an earnest, good-natured excitement behind his words that I appreciated. I quipped back about tearing it off myself for how he spoke to my customers and he laughed so hard he doubled over.

"I like you, bud," he bellowed, slapping me on the back with that meat paddle he calls a palm. "You should come to the wedding!"

And that was it. We were friends. We kept in touch over social media, eventually messaging random thoughts and funny pictures back and forth every day.

Let's just say that I don't play well with others. Never have. Most people aren't worth knowing, let alone trusting. So I was surprised when I told Billy the story about Persephone. Even more surprised that he was understanding. He shared a Daddy Dom meme and we instantly clicked on a deeper level.

Can't help but envy how Amanda, his perfect match, just fell into his lap. They exit the hall and I pat my pocket, springing to the side door to slip around the clotted crowds forming at the doorways.

There was a little girl I quit for, once. Back when I felt important and purposeful. I mattered as Persephone's Daddy. But as some upper management schmuck? Yeah, it's not my calling.

I've been moving through my life like a ghost. The sharp taste of smoke hits my tongue and my body sponges up the rush.

Sweet, sweet nicotine. My only vice.

There's a soft clop of high heels on marble approaching me, stirring me from my haze. I exhale away from the door, braced for a stern talking-to from an older woman. That'd already happened tonight.

"Too handsome for that garbage," she'd said as a gnarled finger poked my arm. Her face broke into crepe paper wrinkles when she smiled and I couldn't help but smile back. Billy's grandma was just as feisty as I'd expected.

The figure that emerges makes me rub my eyes in disbelief. That jet black hair, silky straight. A blood-red dress hugs the curvy, rolling contours of her beautiful figure. The fabric is so dark it's nearly black in the shadows. Glimmering brown eyes, always vigilant and skeptical.

Unless she's with me.

"Jesus Christ..." I say stupidly, the cigarette hanging from my lips.

"Persy, actually," she teases. A flush creeps up her cheeks as she looks me over.

My little princess of darkness. She's cropped her long locks into a sleek, stylish bob, but other than that, she's scarcely aged since I last saw her so many years ago.

Shit. I feel nervous as a schoolboy. Of all the times I'd dreamed of this moment, I'm disastrously unprepared. I draw on my cigarette, praying to the empty sky for some kind of inspiration.

"Thought you quit," she digs playfully, stepping toward me. In the low light, I see a small shimmer resting an inch above that teasing hint of cleavage.

It's the necklace I got her before I left. Knives twist in my heart and gut simultaneously. Fucking end me.

Was I an asshole for breaking things off completely? Absolutely. But at the time, I was sure I was sparing her heartache by allowing her to move on. Neither of us could change our situation, which drew us states apart.

She'd find love again quickly, I was sure of that. I'd lick my wounds on my own time.

I regretted it every fucking day, but I stuck by my choice. Those wounds never quite healed and I decided to cast off the notion of love all together.

"Never had anybody to keep me in line," I say, flicking the ash over the ledge of the landing.

She looks surprised. "...No?"

I shake my head and spy a hint of a smile at the corner of her mouth.

"It's only Mormon girls in Utah," I joke. It's not entirely the truth — Salt Lake is a city like any other. And I've been propositioned by female members more than I'd like to admit.

The gym Barbies aren't for me, though. Like trying to make a meal off of a granola bar.

No, what I want is the full Thanksgiving spread. A woman stacked with curves, her body warm and soft in my hands. Full and luscious as a goddess of old.

That's why I always called Persy by her full name. "A reverse nickname," she used to tease me. But she fully deserves that level of devotion and admiration.

She lets out a small chuckle at my comment. I butt the smoke halfway — suddenly, I'm not jonesing anymore. It's like I've taken my first full breath since we parted ways.

I've missed the strong sense of duty and responsibility I had when she was in my care. My precious, sensitive, sweet girl. Every step I took was for her, to make our lives better. To make myself better for her sake. To be a better Daddy. Without her to nurture, I've wilted into myself.

It's now or never. I extend my hand to her and nod toward the sleek glass doors behind us.

"Don't know about you, but I don't know a single motherfucker in there," I say with a smirk.

"Me neither," she says, shaking her head. Her hair dances back and forth with her movement, reflecting the low light. "Well, I know Amanda, but she's busy, obviously," she tacks on, then bites her lip.

Nerves. I know her well enough to tell. She's in good company there. My heart is pumping so fast I'm sure she must be able to hear it.

Always told myself that a sweet little treasure like her wouldn't be single for long. Told myself she'd find a new, better Daddy to give her the life she deserves. But when she looks up at me with those warm, wide eyes, I see her desire.

At that moment her stomach rumbles. Loudly. And for longer than you'd expect. She grimaces with embarrassment as I use all my might to bite back laughter. She sees the struggle written all over my face and cracks up, egging me on until we're laughing like maniacs.

Thank god that broke the tension.

"C'mon, lets hit the buffet," I say with a knowing smile. She nods eagerly, her smile beaming across her face. It shines so bright it could burn the darkness from the night sky. My heart pangs as I lead her through the crowd, peeking back every so often to see her holding tight with her icy little hand, her eyes trained on me the whole way.

CHAPTER THREE

I swear I float behind William as he leads me by the hand. His grasp is rough and warm and fits just right. When we find a table, I catch a better look at him.

Salt and pepper have crept over his temples and the edges of his beard. He's ditched his Euro mullet for a slicked back, classic style that suits him wonderfully. A wary, distant look is etched into the lines around his eyes. He's dressed in black from head to toe.

Glad to see he's stayed true to his roots. The thought brings a smile to my face. My whole body is fluttering frantically now that I'm near him. Excitement, anxiety, longing and lust swirl in my mind, making me unsteady. We slide along the buffet together and I heap things mindlessly on my dish. Every time our arms brush I'm afraid I'll drop my plate from the jolt.

Just his proximity is making me wet. I'm not sure how I could resist, considering how we used to play...

The memory hits me like a tidal wave. His low growl rumbling through me as he fucked me hard from behind. My red-hot, freshly spanked ass bouncing against him. How hard we came together.

Nope. Not going down that road. I have no idea what his life is like now. He raises a curious eyebrow at my plate before leading me back to the table.

Okay, so I grabbed three dinner rolls, creamed spinach, penne marinara, and chicken fingers. They're mixed together in a hideous pile and I wish the heat in my cheeks would ignite and swallow me in flames.

A moment later, Billy gives me a knowing nod as he carries a huge platter of food with both hands over to the long table where he's seated. Amanda just shakes her head and smiles as he exaggeratedly rubs his belly.

God, they're so in love.

"Good stuff," William says, snapping me back. I work my way around the edges of my plate, tasting the foods on their own and avoiding the big mess in the middle. I'll have to go up by myself and actually pay attention to the next plate.

He's right, though — the food is delicious. Amanda's company catered, so I suppose that makes sense. The food is unpretentious, which adds to the easy, playful atmosphere of the reception.

Amanda changed from her floor-length gown into a short, frilly Lolita dress, white stockings, and white platform sneakers. Yeah, that's way more her.

"How do you know them?" I ask suddenly, the question hitting me over the head like a frying pan.

"Billy came to my gym before a comp in Salt Lake. Couldn't resist the big jerk, frankly," he says with a timid smile. The curling ends of his lips set off fireworks in my stomach.

"Got pretty close. He's a good guy," he says as he brings a forkful to those luscious, full lips.

"...Persephone?"

Oh shit. I watched his lips part around the pasta and completely spaced out. All the blood left my brain and headed directly south, sending a throb between my legs.

Did he say something? Obviously he said something. Shit.

"Sorry, um, what'd you ask?" I ask as I fidget a lock of hair behind my ear.

"What about you?" he asks musingly, his face perfectly placid.

"Oh, um…" I stammer, unsure what to say. It's not my place to share that Amanda's a little and Billy's her Daddy. But William certainly wouldn't judge. The words back up in my throat and I decide I better spit something out.

"A club! We met in a club. Online. For, uh, an interest that we share." Ugh. So smooth. I bring my palm to my forehead and sigh, peeking at William's warm gaze. He can make me feel the sun on my skin with how he looks at me. God, I've missed that.

He nods knowingly with a sly smirk. No doubt he's picked up on my meaning. If he and Billy are close, they've probably talked about it.

"Strange how life threw us together," he ponders aloud. There's a wrinkle in his brow as he stares intently into the distance.

"That's a fucking understatement," I mutter dryly. William barks out a laugh and my skin flushes with heat.

There's too much happening in my mind right now. I'm full of a thousand questions I want to ask about his life, so much I want to tell him. But at the same time, I want to drop it all and just be with him tonight, to savor this amazing surprise and enjoy his company.

I debate telling him how much I've missed him when he extends a hand to me, shaking me from my thoughts.

"Let's dance."

Oh, thank god. Please, anything to keep me from making a

total fool of myself. Though I'm not sure I'll fare much better on the dance floor.

Before, I would have been too shy. Too self-conscious. But I've learned the hard way that the sweetest things in life are fleeting. Tomorrow isn't promised and I won't waste this chance.

William glides me around the floor effortlessly. Wow, that's new. The closest thing to dancing I've ever seen him do is thrash in a mosh pit. Now he's sweeping me around the floor so grace-fully that my missteps seem to fall right in time.

Lead me, my mind yearns as I lean into him. Our bodies press together and my nipples harden, brushing against him with each movement. When I look at up him, the whole world around us fades away.

CHAPTER FOUR

William

Damn, it feels good to have her close again. I'd resigned myself to a life of quiet loneliness but now, with Persephone, my body comes alive. Her body fits into mine like a puzzle piece. My heart stirs and I'm awash in my love for her, strong as the day I left.

I've never stopped loving her. In the back of my mind, I knew that. But now it's alive in the room with us, forcing me to pay attention.

She's still got a healthy appetite, which makes me smile. We take a few breaks from dancing to refuel, especially when dessert comes out. Over cake, she tells me that her aunt Marie passed a couple years back. Poor thing. She's matter of fact about it, but there's a distant pain in her eyes. I share my condolences and she brushes it off, so I don't press it further.

Does this mean she's not tied to the area anymore? That maybe we could be together?

Don't assume she wants you, man. I cast the thoughts aside and focus on enjoying tonight without worrying about what happens next.

We dance all night — sometimes slow, sometimes silly. It's so easy with her. We laugh at one another's ridiculous moves and it hits me that I can't remember the last time I felt so deeply content. It's like we're the only people in the room.

Every so often, she peeks up at me. I pull her close as a ballad plays. The crowd is starting to thin and I sneak a glance at my watch. To my shock, it's nearly midnight.

"I've missed you," she murmurs quietly as the music ebbs.

"I've missed you too," I admit, smoothing her hair as I lean her head onto my chest.

Billy and Amanda are some of the last people dancing. He catches my eye and gives me a knowing nod. That satisfied grin makes me wonder if he somehow had a hand in this. Fucking menace, that's definitely something he'd scheme up.

I look down at Persephone in my arms and it hits me again. I never thought I'd have this opportunity.

And I'm not going to fucking waste it.

"Better call a car," she says with a hint of disappointment and she pulls away, taking my hands in hers.

"I can drive you home if you like." I cringe at the obvious excitement in my voice. I wonder if she's still living in Marie's house.

She nibbles at her lower lip. "I don't know...it's all the way across town. The neighborhood hasn't exactly gotten nicer," she falters, looking down at her toes.

Well. Hardly want to drop her off there now. Girl never did have much sense of self-preservation.

"Want to stay at mine?" Her eyes go wide. "I have a whole suite," I tack on, not wanting to appear presumptuous. Though I'd fuck the daylights out of her without a moment's hesitation, if she asked.

It's been a long, long time, and the beast is railing against its cage. She has a powerful effect on me.

The mix of relief and excitement on her face let me know that my offer is exactly what she wanted. Crafty little girl. She always knew exactly how to wrap me around her finger.

The little flicker in her eye sets me ablaze. She wants me too, so much I can nearly taste it.

"Yes," she says after a beat, nodding eagerly and looking up at me with those warm amber eyes.

Good. I take her hand and open the door to the sleek car I've rented for my stay. When I reach across to buckle her seatbelt, I feel her body bristle against mine. She clears her throat — a tell-tale cue that she's excited, but trying to bite it back.

Memories seep into the edges of my mind. Teasing her wet panties at the movie theater, whispering how I'm going to ravage her as soon as we got home. Swatting her ass in public when she strayed too far from me. Edging her until she was panting and shaking, pleading desperately for permission to come.

I practically choke out the steering wheel driving back to the hotel. Thank fuck it's nearby. My entire body is revved up and my cock is defiantly hard inside my dress pants despite my best attempt to will it away. Every cell in my body is starved and ready to devour her.

I pull the car into the curved drive outside the high-rise hotel and toss the keys to the valet. When she slips her hand in mine, so small and soft, I nearly combust.

The elevator door chimes open and I press the button for the top floor. She sneaks glances at me and I wrap my arm around her, pulling her tight to my side. She shivers and leans closer, wrapping one arm around my waist and lazily running her hand over my midsection.

Both of us are fighting the urge to tear each other's clothes off right here. When the key card beeps and we cross the threshold into the sprawling suite, I set my gaze on Persephone's gorgeous figure. After ten years, I can't stand to wait anymore.

CHAPTER FIVE

Persy

William looks me over with a dark, hungry look. A moment later, he pounces on me and draws me into an intense, passionate kiss.

The door slams closed behind us as I clumsily hop out of my heels and slough my coat off, letting it fall to the floor. I nearly trip over it as we step back and he catches me, holding me steady for a moment before hoisting me up and carrying me to bed.

Fuck, he's strong as ever. I grind onto his hardness as he lays me down gently and positions himself on top of me. My arms and legs are wrapped tight around him, keeping him locked in close to me.

I never want to let him go again.

He tugs off his tie and I reach up to unbutton his dress shirt. Fumbling, my jittery fingers can't slip the small button free. He reaches to the collar and tears the shirt open, sending buttons flying everywhere. I can't help but giggle.

Then he grabs the straps of my dress and tugs it down around my waist, letting my breasts spill free. He growls approvingly as he scans my body, then grasps my breasts firmly. His rough palms knead the sensitive flesh just the way I like, evoking a small cry from my throat.

He rolls the tips of my hardened nipples between his fingers and my clit aches in response. It's as if the touch is cutting right through me, lighting up every nerve.

William rears up and tugs my dress of completely, leaving me in just my black panties and thigh-high stockings.

"Jesus fucking Christ, Persephone," he curses as he ogles me lewdly. The effect on him is clear, which skyrockets my excitement. He looks at me like I'm the most beautiful, desirable creature in the world.

With a growl he kisses down my stomach, gently squeezing the soft flesh. He grunts and sighs as he greedily makes his way down, kissing the seams of my thighs. When his mouth hovers over my slit, kissing gently over the fabric of my panties, I swear the heat alone is nearly enough to make me come.

I'd considered a hookup once after William broke up with me, but I couldn't go through with it. It feels like a lifetime since I've been touched like this.

He tugs my panties roughly to the side and dives onto my mound, lapping ravenously at my clit.

"My little princess," he rumbles as he slides a finger inside. He curls it perfectly, hitting my internal spot with each powerful probe. He licks my clit in time with his movements and my pleasure crests suddenly. The sudden, intense orgasm wrings me dry as powerful, tingling waves crash over me.

The sensation is so intense that I nearly weep. I'm ragged and panting, limp on the bead, drifting in the afterglow.

Uh oh. Before, when we would play, I was only allowed to come with permission. No way the old rules still apply, right?

God, I sure hope they do.

"You remember your safeword?" He asks once I've landed. My breathing hitches in excitement.

"Yes!" I say, so plainly eager that I flush with embarrassment.

Whatever punishment he has in mind, my body is ready for it. Screaming for it.

He trails a finger down the center line of my stomach. "As I recall, little girls are only supposed to come with Daddy's permission." The mischievous note in his voice sets a fire between my legs.

"That's right, Daddy," I reply, hoping to encourage him. My ass is dying for a good, hard spanking.

Heat burns in his gaze. "On your tummy," he commands, tapping the side of my hip.

"Yeah?!" I cry excitedly, scrambling into position.

He chuckles at that. "Yes, baby girl," he whispers in my ear as he rises to stand, running his palm over my lower back.

Fuck, I feel so safe with him. Even with ass poking up over of the edge of the bed, my legs spread wide.

"There's no more beautiful sight in the fucking world than this, right here, sweet girl," he praises as he runs his hands over my soft, round ass. He grabs a handful on each side and squeezes tight, making me moan with lust.

The first few blows are gentle. He's warming me up.

"I'll spank you until I decide you've had enough," he growls as the next spank rings through the room.

His words send a surge through me. Submission sinks me deep into the mattress as I give my body over to him.

He knows exactly how to read me and how my body responds. He'll pull back before I hit my limit, I'm sure of that.

He's always a Daddy first.

The blows are raining down quick and firm, warming my behind until it starts to tingle and sting.

I'm such a little masochist. The gentle pain whets my appetite for more. I want that sweltering, throbbing, searing pain. Crave it, even.

I wiggle a little and grunt in frustration. William responds by clamping a strong, muscular arm over my waist and holding me firmly in place.

"Yes, Daddy!" I wail as the spanks fall harder. Each sharp blow rings through me with a sharp, white-hot sting. Rippling pain ebbs and gives way to warm, melty relaxation. He works back and forth in an even rhythm, making the intoxicating sensations dance and swirl in my body.

He's relentless now, darkening my ass from rosy pink to roaring crimson. My defenses have been worn away and the tears start to well in my eyes.

I cry softly as the pain tears through me. It's cleansing, so intense that it pushes all of the hurt from my insides. Tears streak hot down my face as William delivers the last blow, then rubs my lower back gently.

"How's my good girl?" he coos as he brushes a strand of hair from my face, bending down low to look me over. It's overwhelming to be with him again. Like coming home after a long, tiring trip.

"Ah, good, Daddy," I sniffle. He nods and runs a finger over my drenched slit, making me moan.

The electric sensation pushes the rushing thoughts from my mind.

Thank you, horny brain.

Behind me, I hear the quiet *zzzt* of his zipper and fire blooms on my skin. Fuck, I want him. More than anything.

"D-do you have protection?" I stutter, craning my head up to look at him.

He comes to sit beside me on the bed. Rock hard and naked as a jaybird.

I choke down a swallow at the sight of his thick, hard cock. My body remembers how good he feels inside me.

He pats my behind gently and I move to sit beside him. When my aching ass hits the bed I wince slightly, then settle in.

God, his cock is gorgeous. I reach out to stroke him lazily, making him hiss through clenched teeth.

"You're not on the pill anymore?" he asks breathily, clearly effected by my thumb trailing over the head of his cock.

"I am..." I trail off. I can't bring myself to ask the question burning in my throat.

He clears his throat and lays his hand atop mine to stop my strokes.

"I haven't been with anyone else."

He...what? No. No way that's possible.

"Seriously," he says in response to my gawking expression. My heart skips a beat, then fires in double-time.

"Oh. I, I haven't—um, I mean—" I babble senselessly. Seems I've finally lost my grip on speech entirely.

William ticks an eyebrow up with a worried look. "Woah, okay. Pause." He pulls me down to lay facing him, our faces just inches apart.

Those dark eyes, rich as burnt umber, search my expression. I'm still reeling from his words. Of course I haven't been with anyone else, but I figured he'd be beating them away with a stick.

"N-no one? In all this time?" I blurt out. I got so lost in his eyes that I'm not sure how long we've been laying here.

"No one," he tells me declaratively. Then he adds, "Women have offered, but they did nothing for me. All I felt was longing."

My jaw drops open. Is he telling me…?

"Longing for you," he says, as if he could read my thoughts. "An empty fuck would've just reminded me what I really wanted. Of what I'd let go," he says, his voice strained.

Tears spring to my eyes but this time I let out an ugly sob. I can't believe what I'm hearing.

"Breathe, baby," he cues as he rubs my back slowly.

"Talk to me."

The words pour out of me. I haven't been with anyone either. It was easier to put him out of my mind when I was focused on Auntie, but after she died, the loneliness was overwhelming. I'd thought of reaching out to him but I was sure he'd met someone else. He was such a perfect Daddy, how could he not?

"Perfect for *you*," he chuckles gently when I finish. "I'm hardly perfect. Hell, I couldn't even stay away from cigarettes without my little bloodhound to keep me in line," he says playfully, booping me on the nose.

"Yeah, you're gonna have to knock that shit off," I say sternly before bursting into laughter.

"Yes, boss," he teases.

I nuzzle into his neck and we melt together for a moment. It's like he'd never left.

"I know," he says softly.

"Shit, did I say that out loud?"

"Yes, baby," he replies as he sits up, then pulls me onto his lap.

He takes my chin between his fingers and holds my gaze steady on him.

"You're all I want in this world, Persephone," he says, deadly serious. His words untie knot after knot in my belly, encouraging me to say the words.

"I...I still love you, William," I cry at the admission. Tears start to shine in his earnest, pained eyes and my heart breaks open.

"I love you too, Persephone. Never stopped," he declares before drawing me into a ravenous kiss. I throw my arms around his neck and cling tight as I swing my hips onto him.

From the straddle, I tease his throbbing cock over my entrance before sliding down slowly, crying out with delight as he enters me. I moan into our kiss as the tears roll down my cheeks.

It's an intense pleasure. My heart is full. My soul is whole, overflowing with love. And my pussy is wrapped tight around Daddy's cock.

He holds me hips tight as he thrusts into me, burying himself to the hilt. I roll my hips in time with his strokes and his cock hits every pleasure center inside me.

"I love you, Daddy," I cry desperately as my pleasure builds.

"I love you too, princess," he huffs deeply in my ear.

Heat and pressure start to build low in my belly as my climax edges nearer. He hears my panting, desperate moans and slips a hand between us to stroke my clit as I ride him.

"Ah, Daddy! Please!" I plead as my body starts to tremble. He growls with satisfaction, slamming deep into me with each thrust.

"Come with me, Persephone. Come for Daddy," he roars as we crest together, my body clenching and quaking around him as he pumps me full of hot seed. We shudder as the aftershocks roll through us and I rest myself down on top of him.

After a moment, he softens and plops out with a loud squelch. The sound cracks me up. For our beautiful, soulful reunion, we'd certainly made quite the mess.

"Better clean up," William chuckles, standing me up beside the bed. A deluge of wetness soaks my thighs and I scuttle towards the bathroom. To my surprise, he's following right behind me.

He grabs a rag from beside the sink and runs it under the tap. "Tinkle," he commands, nodding toward the toilet.

I cross my arms over my chest in protest. The full length mirror that runs along the opposite wall lets me know how absolutely ridiculous I look.

When he gives me that stern *or else* glance, I scurry over to do my business. Thankfully the bathroom is large so I'm tucked away from the sink.

Bossy Daddy. His favorite adage is "if you don't pee after you screw, you'll be screwed when you pee."

Fucking smartass. I love him so much.

After I flush, William cleans off the mess between my legs with a warm cloth. It's so tender and gentle, but still makes me blush.

He carries me back to bed and we curl up together. It's so warm here, snuggled up with him. I'm protected. Safe.

In his arms, I feel at home, at long last.

EPILOGUE

It *was* a scheme! Amanda and Billy had planned to reunite us.

Turns out, William had told Billy about me, and of course I'd told Amanda all about him. Those two troublemakers couldn't help themselves. They hatched a plan and gave us both the gift of a lifetime.

Both of us assumed the other had moved on. Instead, we had the sweetest reunion.

We talked long distance for a few weeks until I found a job in Utah. Amanda practically packed my bags for me when I told her I was considering the move.

"What's to fucking consider? You guys are on some star-crossed lover shit. Be with him!" The memory of her words still makes me chuckle.

The plan was for me to "crash" with him until I found my own place after a month or two. Neither of us were surprised when I admitted that I didn't want to leave. He wanted me to stay, too.

The bank job is fine. Midwesterners are a different breed — *really* friendly. Almost aggressively so. And too talkative. Still, it's alright. It reminds me to slow down and appreciate things.

There's so much to be grateful for. The land in Utah is absolutely breathtaking. So different from New York. Bare, huge stone mountains jut defiantly into the wide-open blue sky.

When we're not running around the mountains, William and I spend our time cooking and playing together. Let's just say we have a *lot* of catching up to do in that department. It took a few months for us to settle down and I finally quit walking like a horseback rider.

Tonight is the one year anniversary of our reunion. I'm spiffed up in a silky, pine green dress that swishes around my hips when I move. The Italian takeout I ordered is arranged on the table, filling the house with mouth-watering aromas.

It's probably the makings for a food coma, but it's worth it. We deserve a big celebration.

William strolls through the front door looking like a meal himself. Wow. He wears the shit out of a jacket and tie. He ditches them both and tosses them haphazardly on the sofa.

"This looks wonderful, princess," he murmurs as he plants a kiss on my forehead. He seems distracted, which is odd for him. I brush it off and make him a plate.

We eat together and he says the food is perfect. As he finishes up, I rise to clear the plates but he tells me firmly to stay put.

"Yessir," I mumble facetiously under my breath.

"Heard that," I hear him call from the kitchen. How the hell did he pick that up from in there? Supersonic hearing must be one of his Daddy powers.

I sip a glass of wine and savor how full I feel. My tummy, yes, but also my heart. My whole life. Auntie would be so happy to see me now.

William returns from the kitchen and kneels in front of me. I'm not sure why — there's no shoes to untie. Then he pulls a little box out of his pocket.

Oh. Oh my god.

"Persephone," he says, cracking the box open to reveal a black diamond nestled in a detailed black metal setting.

It couldn't be more perfect.

"I made a mistake letting you go all those years ago. I've regretted it every day." Emotion shines brightly in his eyes and my own tears break free, spilling down my cheeks.

"We got a second chance, and this time, I won't let you slip away. You're my little goddess, Persephone. The jewel of my life. I'm eternally yours." He hovers the wedding band over my ring finger.

"Yes! Yes, yes yes!" I wail, doubling over and wrapping myself around his shoulders. He cups my face and wipes the tears away. Then he slides the ring onto my trembling finger.

"So, will you marry me?" he beams. I let out a laugh, then sniffle.

"Of course."

"I love you, Persephone," he whispers, drawing me up into his arms.

"I love you, too, Daddy," I whimper, burying my face in his neck. No matter what comes our way, we'll face it together. Nothing will tear us apart again.

BOOKS BY THIS AUTHOR

Powering Daddy

Billy is a big boy. Enormous. "Genetically gifted," sportscasters have called him. He's a professional strongman who hires private chef Amanda to cook him six meals a day. She can barely keep up with the voracious appetite of this cocky, arrogant giant. Despite their rough start, Amanda and Billy grow fond of one another. She can't deny her lust for Billy's huge, rippling body. And it turns out Billy's insatiable appetites go way beyond the kitchen. Will Amanda be able to resist the advances of this dominant behemoth? And the bigger question is, will she want to?

Daddy's Security

If you give a brat a curfew, you're going to have to give her some discipline to go with it.

Elle, a spoiled, melancholy starlet, can't believe that gruff Leroy won't bend to her will. Her huge, surly security guard is the first person in her life to give her any boundaries. Or tries to, at least.

When Elle puts herself in danger, Leroy has to grapple with his dominant, Daddy side being pulled to this reckless little girl. Can they deny the magnetism between them? Emotional, raw, and plenty spicy, this quick instalove romance is lavish as the Hollywood Hills.

Papa's Queen

Lady DuFonte is a princess in a cold, lonely tower. Widowed at twenty, she returns to her family in mourning. Her father is eager to marry her off, despite her protest. When she lays eyes on her betrothed — a hulking, fur-clad warrior from the north — she's certain she doesn't have the strength to resist his bestial desires. Will the bold, bawdy Clemont be a brutish or tender with his little princess? The answer shocks her beyond her wildest dreams.

Daddy's Protection

A thief broke into her apartment. Then Roland broke into her heart.

Cam never stood a chance at resisting him. Not with those huge, rippling muscles covered in tattoos. Those dark, searching eyes. He's the hero she least expected, but needed more than anything. There's an effortless chemistry between Cam and Roland that makes her wonder. Could he be the Daddy Dom she's always longed for? Or will he reject her, like the others before, when she shares her little side? Look inside this steamy, instalove, age play romance to find out!

Daddy's Treat

"By now, I release into his touch instinctively. It evokes trust. It reminds me that I'm completely safe, even as I lay here pinned down and spread wide. I'm completely open, but Daddy is in control. I can surrender."

Join established couple Mark and Jules, a Daddy Dom and his little princess, as they celebrate their eight year anniversary. Daddy Mark has some special surprises in store for Jules...something to push her submission even further. Enjoy the deep, complete surrender that only a doting Daddy Dom and provide.

Disciplined By Daddy

I never would have imagined at nineteen that the man across the altar from me would become my Daddy. But that's how our story goes. Ten years later, we live as husband and wife but play like a stern Daddy and his little princess. Take a peek into our steamy romance and how Daddy deals with broken rules. Even over his knee, begging for release, I know I'm his good girl forever.

CLAIM YOUR FREE STORY!

Ani has made a terrible mistake. After breaking one of her longest standing rules with her Daddy, Brady, she confesses everything. Brady is tender and comforting, but stern when it comes to punishment. Join this established, loving DDlg couple for some steamy discipline over Daddy's knee!

Sign up for my newsletter to receive your FREE copy of Ani's Confession! Exclusively for new subscribers!!

THANK YOU FOR READING

Thank you so much for supporting my work. I love writing about this lifestyle and you make it possible!

Want a FREE eBook? Sign up for my newsletter to receive an exclusive story!! Plus sneak-peaks and snippets of my upcoming work! No spam, ever — pinkie swear.

Follow me on Amazon Author Central to stay up to date on my publications!

'Til next time,
Sonia

www.ingramcontent.com/pod-product-compliance
Lightning Source LLC
Chambersburg PA
CBHW071237140726
47996CB00007B/2640